M & M

and

The Super Child Afternoon

By Pat Ross

Pictures by Marylin Hafner

PUFFIN BOOKS

PUFFIN BOOKS

Published by the Penguin Group

Viking Penguin, a division of Penguin Books USA Inc.,

40 West 23rd Street, New York, New York 10010, U.S.A.

Penguin Books Ltd, 27 Wrights Lane, London W8 5TZ, England

Penguin Books Australia Ltd, Ringwood, Victoria, Australia

Penguin Books Canada Ltd, 2801 John Street, Markham, Ontario, Canada L3R 1B4

Penguin Books (N.Z.) Ltd, 182–190 Wairau Road, Auckland 10, New Zealand

Penguin Books Ltd, Registered Offices: Harmondsworth, Middlesex, England

First published in the United States of America by Viking Penguin,

a division of Penguin Books USA Inc., 1987

Published in Puffin Books, 1989

1 3 5 7 9 10 8 6 4 2

LIBRARY OF CONGRESS CATALOGING-IN-PUBLICATION DATA

Ross, Pat.

M & M and the super child afternoon / by Pat Ross ;

pictures by Marylin Hafner.   p.   cm.   "Puffin books."

Summary: When best friends Mimi and Mandy turn out to be more

talented at each other's special choice in a "Super Child" class,

they decide to go their separate ways after school.

ISBN 0-14-032145-4

[1. Friendship—Fiction.   2. Schools—Fiction.]   I. Hafner, Marylin, ill.

II. Title.   III. Title: M and M and the super child afternoon.

PZ7.R71973Mc   1989   [E]—dc19   89-5416

Printed in the United States of America

by R. R. Donnelley & Sons, Harrisonburg, Virginia

Set in Times Roman

Finally, one for Hilary

1.
A New Sign

There was a brand-new sign in the grocery store window. Mandy and Mimi, the friends M and M, stopped to look.

The paint was fresh and bright. And the sign said:

SUPERCHILD AFTERNOON!
EVERY WEDNESDAY AT
—3—
at the EAST END CENTER.
Choose from Many Exciting
CLASSES.
→ SIGN UP TODAY ←
YOU Can be a SUPERCHILD!
DEVELOP YOUR TALENTS NOW!

"Wow, I'd really like to be a Super Child," said Mimi.

"Me, too!" said Mandy. "Let's sign up together."

"You bet!" agreed Mimi.

They looked at the long list of classes. It would be hard to choose just one.

First came TENNIS.

Mandy and Mimi both knew that tennis was a good game for two friends.

They both had sneakers.

But they needed tennis rackets.

So they went to the next: CREATIVE MOVEMENT.

"That sounds dumb," said Mimi. "Let's skip it."

Then came VOLLEYBALL.

"All the big kids will sign up for that one. They'll cream us," said Mandy.

"So much for volleyball," agreed Mimi.

They said no to CHESS ("Too slow!"),
PHOTOGRAPHY ("Boring!"), FINGER
PAINTING ("For babies!"), and POTTERY
("Very messy!"), and maybe to PING-
PONG and BASKETBALL.

Finally they came to a class that was
something Mandy had always wanted to
do, ever since she was old enough to
stand on her tiptoes. It was BALLET.

"Look!" she cried, and pointed. "That's a good one. For *both* of us," she added, hoping Mimi would agree.

Mandy closed her eyes. She saw herself twirling and leaping in bright pink tights and little black slippers in the Super Child Afternoon's ballet class.

She knew in her heart that she would be graceful and so light on her feet. And now was the chance to prove it!

"Look!" cried Mimi.

Now *Mimi* was pointing to something on the sign. But she wasn't pointing to BALLET. She was pointing to GYMNASTICS.

The big G in GYMNASTICS reminded Mimi of the way she would stretch and twist if she could take gymnastics.

Already she could turn a cartwheel on her living-room rug. Now she could imagine herself turning one, then two, then three cartwheels in a row and not getting dizzy.

Mimi just knew she'd be able to stand on her head, too. She was sure gymnastics was her true talent. If only Mandy would say yes.

There were no more classes left on the list now. Mandy and Mimi looked at each other.

"What do you think?" asked Mimi.

"Ballet," said Mandy. Mandy could feel her toes begin to curl. "What do *you* think?" asked Mandy.

"Gymnastics," said Mimi.

Right away, the friends M and M could tell they had a problem.

"Ballet is better," said Mandy, talking faster now. "There's music and tights and toe shoes and tutus in nice colors. Gymnastics is just hot and sweaty."

"Gymnastics is good for you," said Mimi, feeling stubborn now. "And it's just as pretty. You can do cartwheels and splits. You can be in the Olympics! Ballet is just silly."

And then the fight began!

"Ballet!" yelled Mandy.

"Gymnastics!" yelled Mimi.

Finally, Mandy said, "Would you try ballet? Then you'll see ballet is best."

"I'll try ballet," said Mimi, "if you'll try gymnastics. Then you'll see that gymnastics is better."

So they shook on it. First they would
try ballet together. Then they would try
gymnastics. After that, they would choose
one. It was only fair. And it was the only
way if they were going to be in the Super
Child Afternoon together.

2.
Ballet

The people at the East End Center said it was okay to try each class once. Since B came before G, Mandy and Mimi decided to try ballet first.

Mimi was very grumpy in the locker room. Her old tights were too short. She had lost her only headband. And her leotard had dried spaghetti sauce all down the front. She walked to class behind Mandy feeling stupid.

Mandy was feeling great. Her mother had bought her a new leotard with tights to match. By the second class, she would have real ballet slippers with little elastic straps. Her hair was pulled back into a neat ponytail.

The class lined up, one behind the other, along the wall.

Mandy looked in the mirror. *I look like a real dancer,* she thought.

Mimi could not stand to look at herself in the mirror. And there were mirrors everywhere! Her hair kept falling in her eyes. She looked like a dancing dog, not a ballerina.

When the teacher wasn't looking, Mimi whispered to Mandy, "This is a big mistake!" Mandy pretended she had not heard.

Soon it was time to begin. "Follow me," said the teacher, who was lovely and graceful. "And follow the music. . . . Begin."

A quick little tune came from the piano.

Mandy knew that it was time for her to show everyone how lovely and graceful she could be.

She spread her arms wide and put her feet in first position, just like the teacher. Then she tried to bend her knees and sink down slowly, keeping time to the music. First she wobbled, then she slipped. Then she sat down hard—*plop*!

"Try again," said the teacher, who wasn't very helpful.

When Mimi heard the music, she spread her arms wide and said to herself, "Here goes nothing!" Then she bent her knees slowly, in time to the music. Mimi's back was straight, and her balance was perfect. She did it again, and again.

"Very good plié!" said the teacher.

"I thought you hated ballet,"
whispered Mandy.

"No talking, children," scolded the
teacher. "We're going on to something
harder now. Please watch me carefully.
Then we'll go one at a time."

*Maybe first position was just too easy
for someone like me*, thought Mandy.

The something harder was point, turn,
point, across the floor. You had to twirl
a little on the turn, and that thrilled
Mandy.

The music started again. It was the
same quick little tune.

"I'm getting sick of that song,"
groaned Mandy.

"I'm starting to like it," said Mimi.

"We'll begin with you," said the teacher. She was pointing to Mandy.

Mandy stood tall and pointed her toe. That went okay. *Now for the twirl,* thought Mandy eagerly. She swung her body and her arms, but her feet forgot to keep up. *Point, turn, point, clunk, clunk, clunk!* went Mandy.

When Mandy looked in the tall mirror, she thought she saw a duck, not a graceful ballerina.

"Keep trying," said the teacher.

Finally it was Mimi's turn to go. She brushed the hair out of her face and took a deep breath. ''Ready, set, go,'' she said to herself.

When Mimi pointed her foot, it looked straight and perfect. When she turned and twirled slightly, everyone in the class made an ''ahhh'' sound.

''Again!'' cried the teacher.

So Mimi did points and turns again and again across the floor. Her balance was perfect. Her body was graceful. And no one paid attention to the spaghetti dribble on her leotard.

"Very good!" said the teacher. "Please line up in rows now, class. Come to the front, dear," she said to Mimi.

Mimi moved to the front of the class, pleased and surprised that she was so good at ballet. *Well*, she thought, *if I'm this good at ballet, I'll be great at gymnastics.*

Mandy felt awful. She moved to the back of the room so Mimi wouldn't see her cry. For the rest of the class, she tried to keep up. But her feet just wouldn't follow. The music sounded too fast. Now she really hated that little tune!

If I'm this awful at ballet, she thought, *I'll be even worse at gymnastics. And Mimi won't want to be friends with a failure.*

All the next week, Mimi twirled around the room. And Mandy practiced standing on her head. Gymnastics was next.

3.
Gymnastics

The locker room was crowded. It looked as if everyone had signed up for gymnastics. Mandy and Mimi had to share a locker.

Quickly, Mimi put on her favorite blue shorts. Then she pulled her lucky T-shirt out of her gym bag. It said SEA WORLD and had a picture of a killer whale on the front. Mimi had brought two headbands, a sweatband, and two wristbands. This was the class she had waited for!

Mandy took her time getting dressed. Her shorts were baggy. Her plain white T-shirt had shrunk in the wash. She had lost her only barrette. She wished she had a stomachache or a broken leg. Then she could go home sick.

"Here," said Mimi, handing Mandy her extra headband.

"Thanks," said Mandy.

In the gymnasium groups of kids tumbled on the mats and warmed up. Mimi joined right in. Mandy sat in the corner.

''Warm-up time!'' cried the gym teacher over the noise. Then he blew his whistle to line up.

Mimi was sure gymnastics would be easy. She felt tough and strong and ready for anything.

First they did jumping jacks. Then they did running in place. Then they did sit-ups.

Mimi puffed and she panted. She felt awful, but she didn't give up. "This is some workout!" Mimi whispered to Mandy.

Mandy puffed and she panted. But she felt great. She even felt ready now for the gymnastics part. "This is easier than I thought," she said to Mimi.

"Okay! Let's see your cartwheels," shouted the gym teacher.

This was the moment that Mimi had been waiting for. It looked so easy to do cartwheels across the gym, like an Olympic athlete. The mat felt soft and spongy under her feet—almost as soft as her living-room rug. She was ready.

"Next," said the teacher.

Mimi took a deep breath, and she did her best cartwheel. But it was more like a big *plunk* on the mat.

"You need more lift there," said the teacher. "Now let's see a headstand."

Mimi got one leg up. *I'm going to be great!* she thought. Then she wobbled. Her legs twirled like propellers. Finally she landed in a belly flop on the mat.

"That needs work," said the teacher. "Next."

It was Mandy's turn. She had watched
Mimi and she was scared. If Mimi
wobbled and fell, how would she even get
off the ground?

"Next," said the teacher again.

Mandy rubbed her legs.

"Ready?" asked the teacher.

"I've got a cramp," Mandy lied.

"You can sit it out," said the teacher.

"No," cried Mandy bravely, "I'm O.K."

Mandy took a deep breath. Then she
took off. Her cartwheel was high and
long. When her legs hit the ground, she
didn't wait to begin another. Cartwheels
felt so right that Mandy did five.

"Not bad!" said the teacher. "Now
let's see your headstand."

Mandy had been practicing standing on her head all week. *Zip! Zip!* Her legs went up, and she stayed on her head till the teacher made her come down.

"Not bad," he said again, and the way he said it told Mandy she had been terrific.

For the rest of the class, Mandy was strong and quick. She didn't feel so bad about ballet now. Gymnastics made her feel great, just the way that Mimi said it would. Mimi would be happy when she told her that gymnastics was for her, too.

For the rest of the class, Mimi tried her best. But she still flopped on her cartwheels. And even her somersaults were crooked and slow. Gymnastics was work, she thought, and not the kind of work she wanted! She thought back to ballet class. She thought about how much fun that was. Well, she *did* like ballet better! Mandy would be glad to hear that.

After class, the friends M and M went back to the locker room. They were ready to choose now—ballet or gymnastics.

4.

Ballet or Gymnastics?

"Okay," said Mimi, feeling hot and sweaty. "You were right all along." She took a deep breath. "Ballet wins. Ballet is definitely better."

Mimi was sure Mandy felt the same way. But a strange little feeling and the look on Mandy's face told her she was wrong.

"No," Mandy said. "Gymnastics is better—for me. But ballet is better—for you."

All the kids in the locker room were laughing and yelling. All except the friends M and M, who looked upset and sad. They were right back where they had started, still wanting to do something together. The Super Child Afternoon suddenly seemed like a bad idea.

Soon all the other children had gone home. The locker room smelled like old socks on a rainy day, but it was a quiet place for friends to talk.

Mandy and Mimi sat on the locker-room floor. They talked about their good times together. They talked about The Haunted House Game they had invented.

"Remember the spiders?" said Mimi.

They talked about the Saturday they got caught in a mummy mess at the museum.

"Remember when we lost the shopping list?" burst out Mimi, remembering their first trip to the grocery store.

"Remember the secrets we told Santa?" Mandy asked. They talked about the bad-news twins they baby-sat for.

They remembered their fights. They remembered making up, because friends like Mandy and Mimi are never enemies for very long.

"I still want to be a Super Child," said Mandy, thinking of her cartwheels.

"Me, too," said Mimi, thinking of her pirouettes. "But I still want to be your friend."

Finally the friends thought of a way they wouldn't have to choose between ballet and gymnastics and being together.

"We'll come together," said Mimi.

"And we'll leave together," said Mandy.

But, in between, one would take ballet and one would take gymnastics.

"Why didn't we think of that before?" they wondered.

Mandy dug deep in her gym bag. She
pulled out her new tights. "You can have
these" she said.

In exchange, Mimi gave Mandy her
wristbands. "You can keep my headband,
too," said Mimi.

Then the two friends slammed their
lockers and zipped up their bags. The
Super Child Afternoon friends were
ready to go home—together.

Don't miss Mandy and Mimi's other funny
troubles in: